Maybe
She Forgot

Maybe
She Forgot

WRITTEN AND ILLUSTRATED
by Ellen Kandoian

COBBLEHILL BOOKS/Dutton • New York

Library of Congress Cataloging-in-Publication Data

Kandoian, Ellen.
Maybe she forgot / written and illustrated by Ellen Kandoian.
p.   cm.
Summary: When her mother is late picking her up from
dance class, Jessie fears that she has been forgotten.
ISBN 0-525-65031-8
[1. Separation anxiety—Fiction.
2. Mothers and daughters—Fiction.]   I. Title.
PZ7.K1274May   1990
[E]—dc20   89-25271
CIP
AC

Published in the United States by
Cobblehill Books,
an affiliate of Dutton Children's Books,
a division of Penguin Books USA Inc.

Typography and jacket design by Kathleen Westray
Printed in Hong Kong
First edition

10 9 8 7 6 5 4 3 2

Dedicated to children who wait

The first day of dance class.

At five o'clock, it's time to go home.

Jessie is the first one ready.

"Time to go get Jessie now."

"I'll be out of your way in a few minutes, ma'am."

Some of the mothers and fathers are already waiting.

Crunch!

It's way past five o'clock now.

Maybe she forgot.

"Jessie, are you still here?"

"I'm waiting for my mother. She's
supposed to come for me."

"Let's try to telephone her. Can
you remember the number?"

Ring, ring, ring, ring, ring, ring, ring.

"I'm afraid maybe she forgot."

"JESSIE!"

"I could never forget about you!"